MW01622932

The Otherworldly Journal
of
Doctor Erasmus Gray

Presented with a foreword by

Jeremy Robinson

FOREWORD

While I am not the author of this curious tome packed with frantic scribblings and inserted illustrations, I received the original via a recent friend, whose many journeys through dimensions of reality will one day be legendary. But we're not here to bolster the reputation of Mr. Milos Vesely. We are here to bear witness.

Humankind has always strived to explore. It's in our DNA. During times primeval, the discovery of a new valley or river might have been enough to satiate the urge. Later, new continents. The Moon and Mars. And then far, far beyond, until humanity was no longer happy finding planets barren of life, or those capable of supporting it but never getting whatever supernatural spark generates that first fragile cell.

It was during this time into which Doctor Erasmus Gray was born, raised, schooled, and unleashed. As can be seen in the pages to follow, his artistic skill, imagination, and fanciful musings are entertaining on their own, but it's his thirst for discovery that is most compelling. Unsatisfied with the desolate universe, he sought just one elusive prize: life.

He pursued it across the galaxy.

Into the waters of another planet, where he lived on a floating habitat.

And into the murky depths never before seen by human eyes.

That is, until it also pursued him.

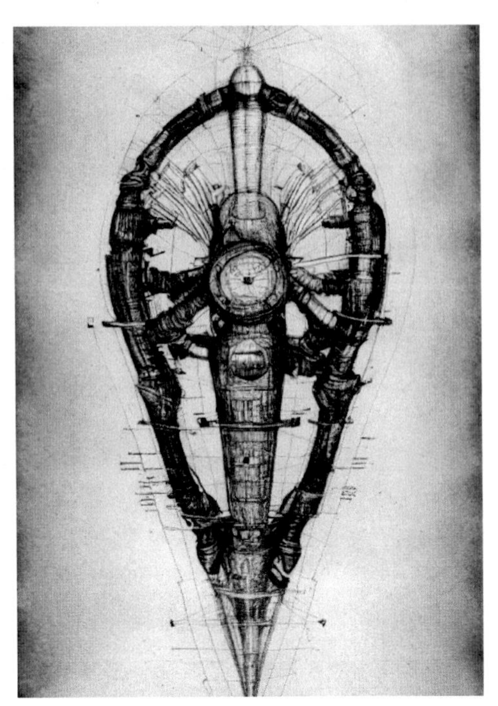

What follows is the only remaining evidence of his future life, in a time beyond imagining, with technology beyond comprehension, stylized after the fictional explorer: Captain Nemo. Gray's journal is full of rare discoveries, an Earth-shattering hypothesis, love lost, and the plight of all humanity: the end.

I hope you enjoy this plunge into a world of pure wonderment, and that it either satiates...or inspires, your own itch to discover.

—Jeremy Robinson

The Otherworldly Journal
of
Doctor Erasmus Gray

Purpose: My first day on S21-B was spent running a systems check on the hab. I am happy to report there are no problems, and my thirty-day voyage into the unknown is off to a splendid start. Although the majority of my notes will be recorded digitally, I will be keeping a journal of brief observations and personal notes, as I do enjoy sketching in my free time. Perhaps this record will be a gift for my dear Delilu, when we are reunited in two months hence. Until that time, I shall do my best to listen, watch, and record what is discovered on this untouched world, even if it is nothing at all. But if it is not... If these pages should miraculously find themselves rife with imagery? Rejoice, for it means life abounds in what was believed to be a barren universe. Now, onward.

Observations: Unable to sleep, I took a water sample and placed a single drop on the glass of a microscope. Imagine my astonishment upon finding a complex, multi-cellular, microbial worm encased in what appears to be a jointed carapace. Thin filaments wriggle from what I believe is the creature's head, perhaps capturing nutrients for sustenance, or possibly functioning as a rudimentary sensory organ. It is difficult to say at this time.

Personal Notes: I am beyond myself with excitement. Sleep will be a long time coming, I imagine. Perhaps days. I have been here for a day, and the universe is already changed forever.

Observations: Today, a mollusk-like creature...not under the microscope. I was able to see this fingernail-sized invertebrate with the naked eye. Reminiscent of the sand flea, this creature could swim quite quickly for its size, moving backward through the water. Or, what I think is backward. I see what looks like two eyes at the base of the creature's skull, giving it literal eyes in the back of its head. Staggering.

Personal Notes: I was taken aback by finding something so large after a night of observing this planet's bounty of microbial life. I suspected, for a brief time, that this planet had yet to evolve beyond the microscopic, but this strange fellow gives me hope that there are more discoveries to come.

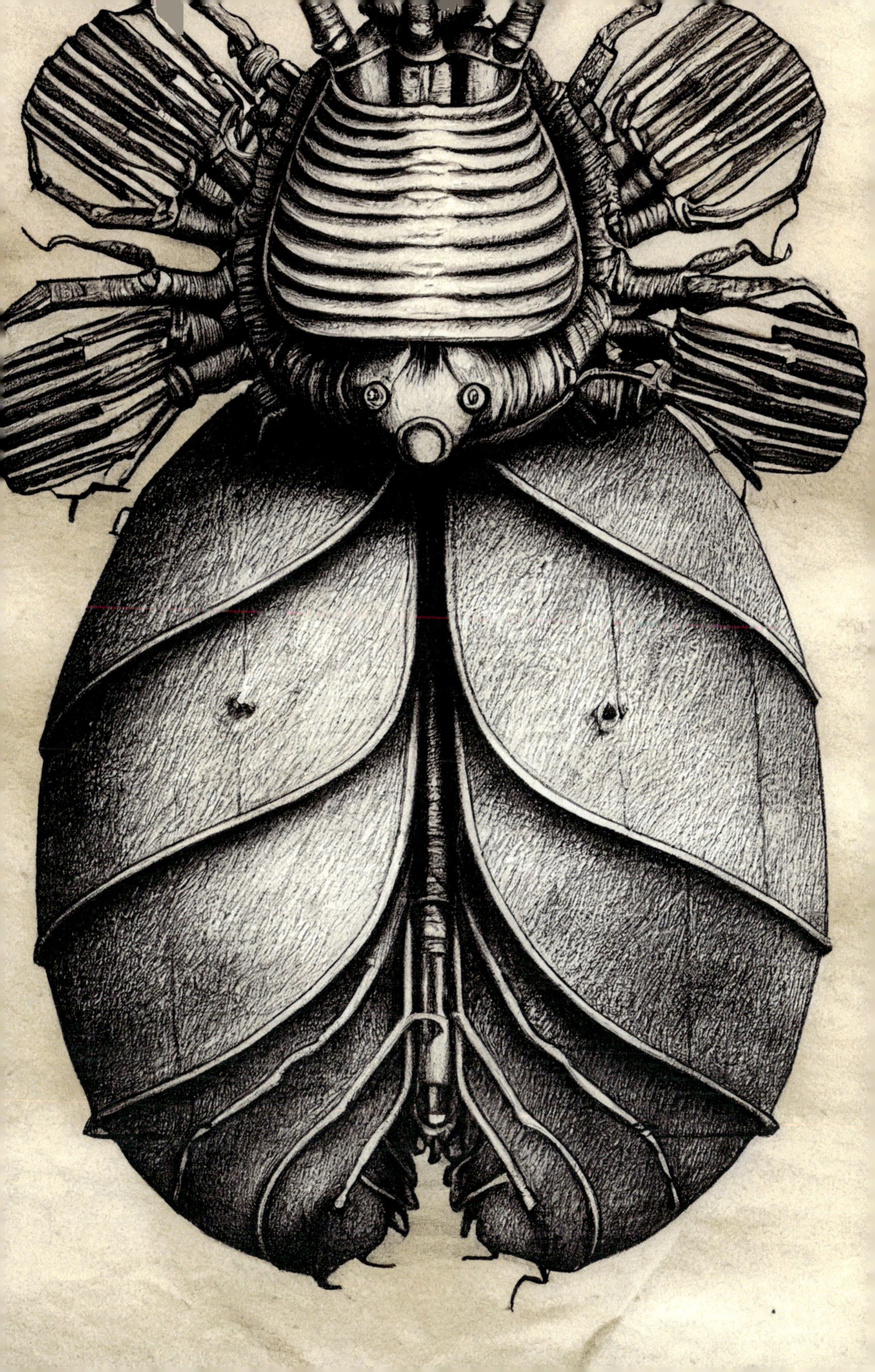

Observations: Lacking any kind of external mobility that I witnessed, this oddity was found floating past the hab. Its features are confounding. Almost mechanical, like an old motor, wrapped in wire...but composed of flesh and bone. Perhaps an ornate shell. I cannot guess. I will eventually need to study the insides of a find, but I am not prepared to start cutting things open. Having just arrived on this world, discovering life, such a thing smacks of barbarism.

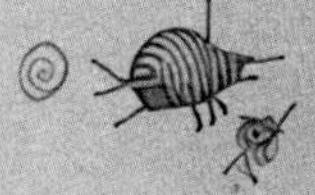

Observations: I was able to launch the ROV today, descending a thousand feet into the depths beneath my meager dwelling. The floating habitat that has become my home is functional, yet cramped. I must strive to keep the living spaces clean and the limited appliances functional. Were I to lose the water purifier, I would have to take my chances with this planet's microbes. The outer deck is a welcome escape—thanks to a breathable atmosphere—allowing me to stretch my legs along the forty feet of catwalk surrounding the square periphery, or to have a lie down atop the roof, watching the strange pink clouds.

Although this was a test run of the vehicle, allowing me to acclimate to the sleek machine's thrusters, as well as its many arms and instruments, I could not resist collecting this deceased specimen. What, at first sight, appeared to be predator and prey, locked together in death, I now suspect might be two members of the same species—though vastly different—tangled in a kind of terminal mating. While I cannot be positive, the wanderings of my imagination lead me to wonder if the young develop in the female of the species, consuming her insides, as they emerge and then feed on the father. The process would be...tragic and beautiful. Parents giving their lives to ensure the well-being of their children. I hope to do the same someday.

Personal Notes: I have clearly begun to miss the presence of Delilu. Perhaps I will draw her soon.

Observations: Another recovery from the ocean floor. I can no longer deny that life on this planet has developed in a way that mimics old Earth machinery. This biomechanical creature stood on the seabed, swaying with the current, the sphincter-like apparatus atop its 'cranium' continuously pulsing in and out, filtering the abundant life from the water. I do not understand the purpose of the rigid, jutting gears and blades, for lack of better words, but I think it wise if I stop viewing this world through the lens of humanity. The lifeforms on this planet clearly operate under different rules.

Personal Notes: Despite rampant discovery, I find myself feeling oddly depressed at the day's end. I believe I might require more sleep.

Observations: Found scuttling along the sand, I mistook this specimen for a human skull...with a tail. When I recovered from my shock, I saw the creature for what it was—a biomechanical crustacean. To my eye, the crab-like organism looks as though it is composed of bits and pieces from a scrapyard, but I am convinced life on this world has simply evolved to appear as machinery. I imagine that to them, they look quite normal, and I am the aberration. A creature without rings, gizmos, and elaborate tubing must look quite peculiar to the denizens of these waters.

Personal Notes: Sleep eludes me still. I fear it will affect my research. I will begin treating the condition of my overstimulated mind tonight, first with meditation and supplements. If that approach does not work, I will resort to synthetics, even though Delilu would not approve.

Apologies, my love. My work here must persist.

Observations: A simple dissection today, of a creature that I believe recently passed and had yet to be discovered by scavengers. This worm-like arthropod, covered in an exoskeleton of ribs is quite sturdy. At first glance it appears as though it might slither along the sandy bottom, but I believe the creature used its six small legs to scurry along, as I have positioned in my sketch. The head came free quite easily, connected to the more well-protected body's flexible flesh. I believe, when in danger, this specimen would be able to retract its body—front and back—into the protective ribs.

Personal Notes: Tired.

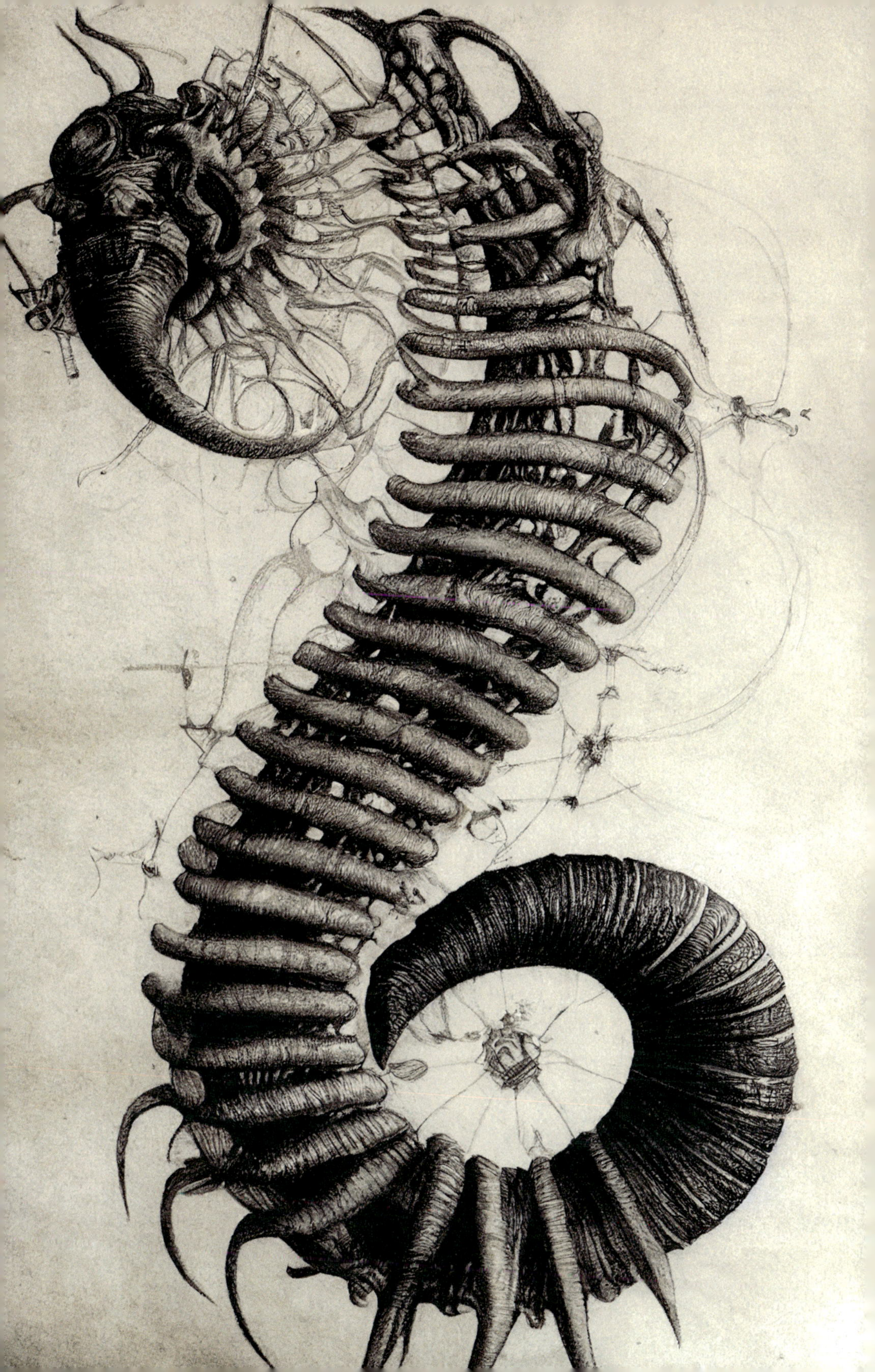

Observations: I know what I am seeing, but I do not understand it. This gelatinous creature...is a jelly fish. An easy to identify species, as it has become so common in the Earth's seas as to become a nuisance. And yet, while recognizable, this specimen is also different. Of this world. Hints of biomechanics mingle with jelly and tendrils. It swam past a portal window as this planet's star fell beyond the horizon. Orange light radiated straight through the organism's transparent hood. I wish you could have seen it.

Personal Notes: Natural remedies have failed. Tonight, I will sleep. Science guarantees it. Forgive me, love, I fear I will soon begin to see things that are not physically present, and in this magical place, I might not be able to tell the difference.

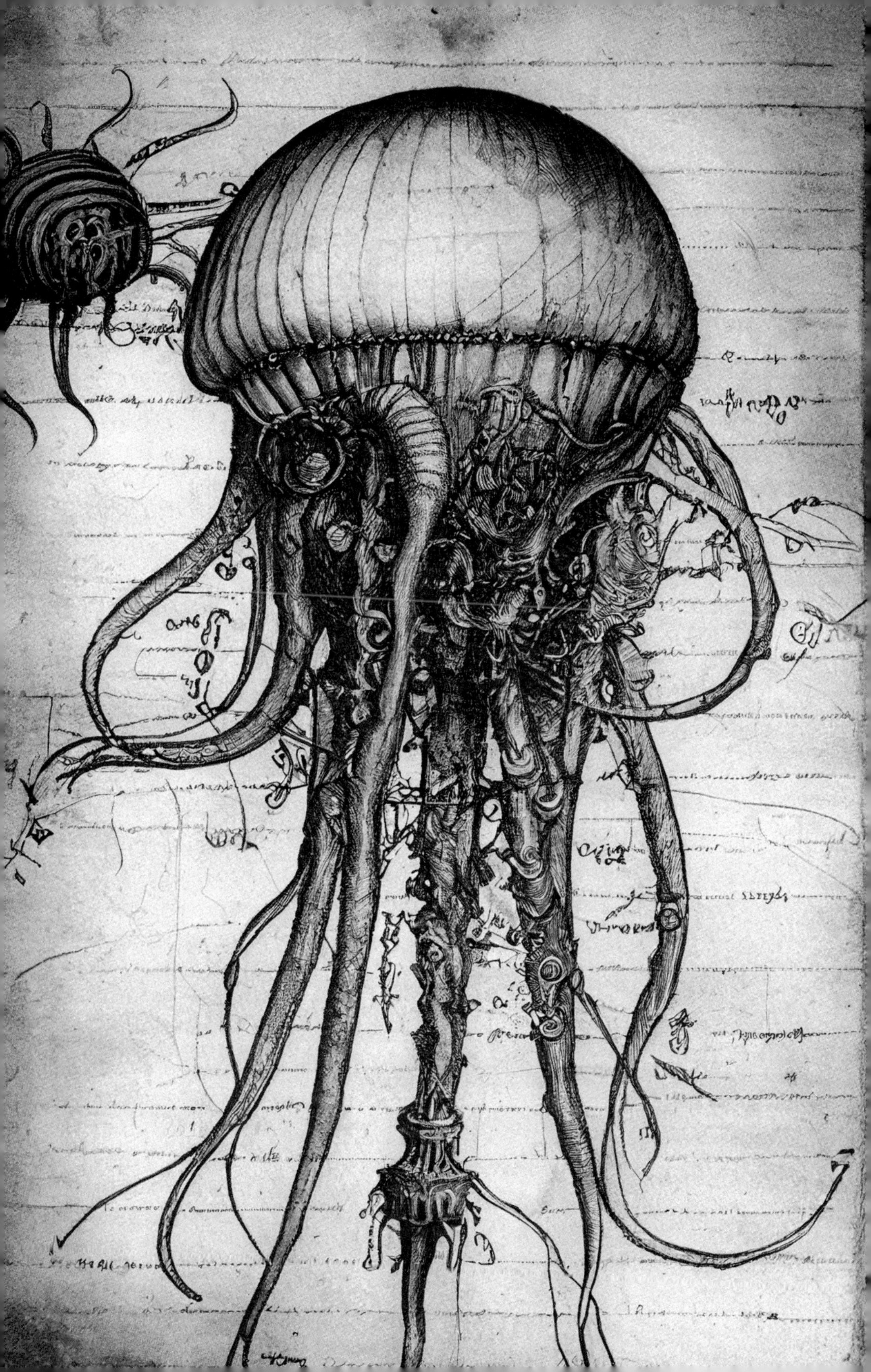

Observations: The sixteen limbs on this mechanical arthropod are only its second most stunning feature. The biomechanical joints, gears, and mechanisms on this creature are not static, as they have been with other specimens. Instead, when this marine animal bustles about its business, the whole core is in motion, spinning gears and all. A wonder to behold, and far too quick for the ROV to catch.

Personal Notes: I slept. Finally. Though I am quite groggy today, either from the many days without sleep, or from the solution itself. Ultimately, it matters not. As long as my work is able to continue. Perhaps I will attempt sleep on my own when my sense of wonder over this place ebbs. Though I do not see how such a thing is possible.

Observations: At first glance, I believed this specimen to be an ocean floor dweller. Like so many others, its body moved with the water. But as the ROV grew near, the hovering appendage filled with some form of gas and lifted toward the surface, pulling what appeared to be a second animal up out of the sand! Once free, the second creature swam, tail moving horizontally, like a fish. It moved away and up at a high rate of speed and has not been spotted since. I believe it had sensory organs atop its fleshy lookout tower. When it detected danger, the gas was released, and action taken. The process was astounding to watch, and I must admit it made me yelp in surprise.

Personal Notes: Sleep continues. I am feeling more like myself, perhaps for the first time since arriving on this world. This sense of normalcy is refreshing, but along with it comes certain longings. My discomfort in combination with constant revelation has served as a substantial distraction from matters of the heart.

Observations: Another jelly. If not for the impossibility that a creature evolved nearly identically on two different planets, I would be bored looking at it. I have seen my fair share. This specimen pulsed past the portal window on the floor of the hab beside my bed. I woke up to it, watched the creature's passage, and then began drawing. Though my sketch is similar in size to others, the total dimensions of this fellow were a little larger than that of my hand. Of all the creatures I have observed thus far, it is the least remarkable—and yet it represents the most inexplicable mystery. Why is this here?

Personal Notes: Flummoxed. Does life evolve along paths predetermined by some cosmic blueprint? Should I expect to find fish? Sea mammals? Turtles? Questions abound, and I am now reconsidering the nature of my previous discoveries. With the mind open to the possibility that evolution is not random, I can see traces of Earth life in everything discovered until now.

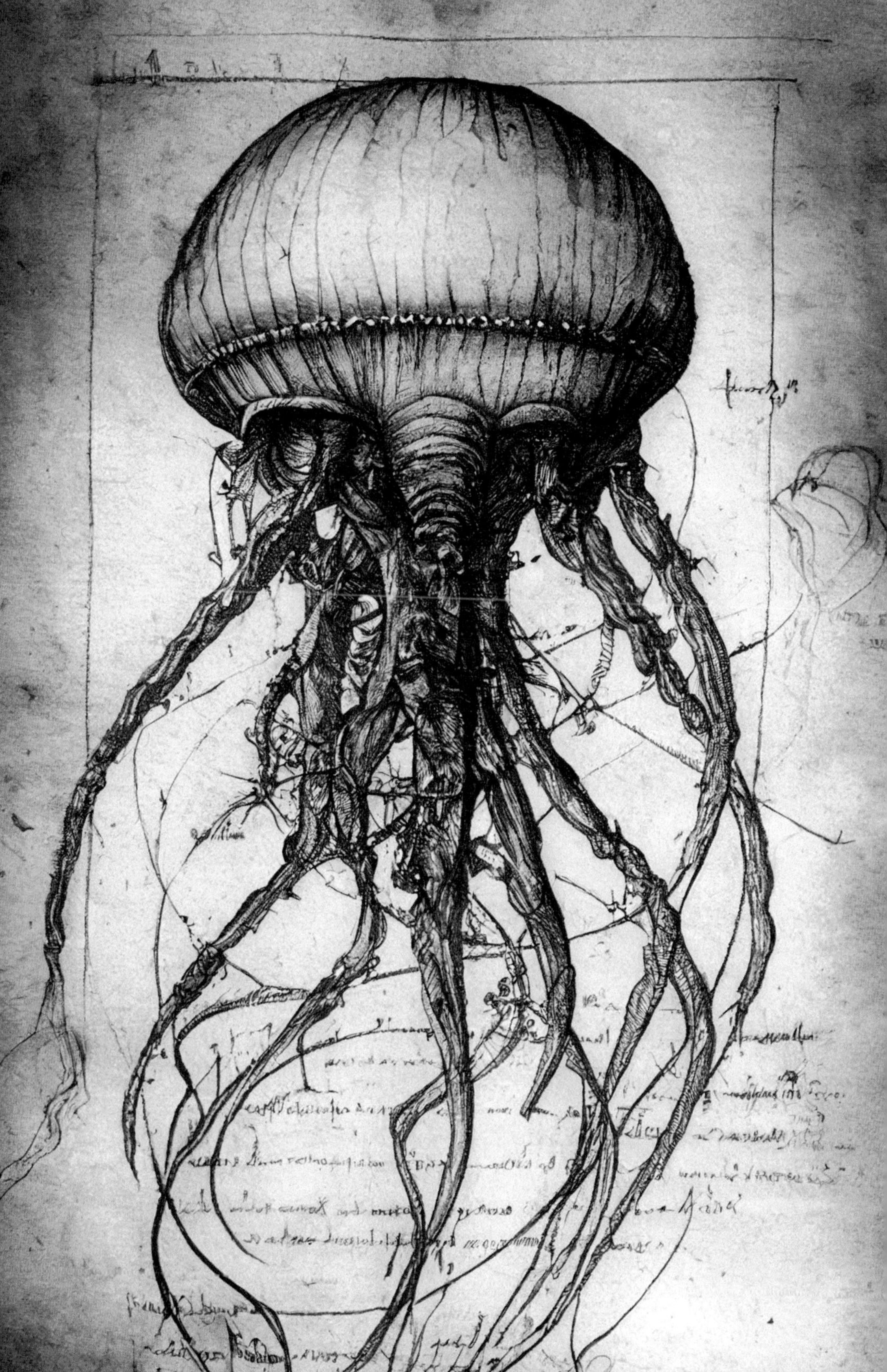

Observations: I have found a living specimen of the merged male and female species, already locked in a coital suicide pact. The male appears almost jubilant in his success. The female of the species is indifferent. I am not even sure she is capable of locomotion. Of peculiar interest is the size and flexibility of the male's...pendulous member. I imagine the ratio of its body size to the dimensions of its reproductive organ to be among the most impressive in the universe. Also of note is that, though living, the female of the species has been previously injured, the shell cracked. I let this pair go that they might complete their perilous coupling.

Personal Notes: Thinking of this mating pair has turned my thoughts back to Delilu. She would redden at the mention of such a thing, but I cannot deny I feel some jealousy, that these creatures have the embrace of another, while my sole company is that of my next drawing.

Observations: This...this is Leopold. All I can discern about my new friend, plucked from the ocean's floor and relocated to one of the holding tanks, is that he is alive. Whether he be plant or animal, I am unsure. There are biomechanical elements and a growth that resembles a bird's skull. It is not unusual for living things to mimic dangerous creatures, thereby scaring off threats. But there are no birds on this world. No flying creatures at all. Without a trace of land marring the perfect blue sphere of this planet, they would have nowhere to roost. Thus, I must chock it up to pareidolia.

Personal Notes: Delilu, pareidolia is the habit of humans to bestow meaning or a biased interpretation of meaningless, coincidental, and random stimuli. Such as seeing the face of a man in the profile of a cliff. Or the curve of a woman in desert sands, wood grain, or just about anything else that slopes downward and crests back up to a smooth curve. We are truly the baser of the sexes. I hope this makes you smile.

Observations: I watched these two...for lack of a better word...fish, swimming around the ROV today. They were inquisitive, if not playful. Curious about every nook and cranny. Their colorations were primal, beiges and browns, striped to camouflage their bodies amidst the craggy stone formations. One appeared quite happy with his lot in life. The other wore a perpetual frown. I do not think they are the same species, but I like to think they are friends. Though they swam with fluid grace, their bodies appear quite rigid, and their eyes smack of mechanical gizmos. I am assuming they can see, but not through any biological mechanism that I recognize.

Personal Notes: Leopold is dead, and I find myself moved to tears by his passing. He kept me company for only a day, but he was a good listener. Side note: his body quickly turned into a viscous glob that broke apart into small pieces. When I poured his remains into the vast sea, the bits were set upon by a shoal of tiny creatures I could not see well enough to draw.

Observations: This appendage was found bouncing along the ocean floor, detached from whatever creature to which it once belonged. It bears a striking resemblance to the limb of an Earth cephalopod, but like everything else here, it is biomechanical in nature, and it appears to be cleanly detached from the creature's body, almost as though designed to break free. On Earth, I would surmise it was a defense mechanism meant to satiate a predator while a hasty retreat was made. But I can assume nothing here. Until I witness such behavior in person, my guesses are just that. On a curious note, the limb was ignored by scavengers and showed no signs of attack. Almost as if it was being avoided.

Personal Notes: Nothing today. Getting the work done. Nose to the grindstone, and all of that.

Observations: I made a new friend. I have named him Gerald. Upon splashing this world's water on my skin for the first time—to see if I would react to it, despite all indications that it was safe—this little scamp came for a visit. At first, he was hesitant, but he responded to my tapping on the water's surface. About the size of my index finger, he began to swim in circles, leaping from the water and extending the fan on his head. The wind would flip him over, and he would plunge back into the endless blue. A one-man show for a one-man audience. When I placed my hand in the water, we chased each other back and forth for some time, and then, miracles of all miracles, he scooted into my palm. For the first time in human history, one of many such claims I can make, a human has made physical contact with a being from another world. After two hours, Gerald had tired of my attention and retreated to the depths.

Personal Notes: Delilu, after two days of reflection, I believe my comments about pareidolia may have come across as sexist. As you are aware, I believe you to be one of the most learned, well-read, and intellectually stimulating women in the known universe. Forgive me for assuming you were unaware of the term's meaning.

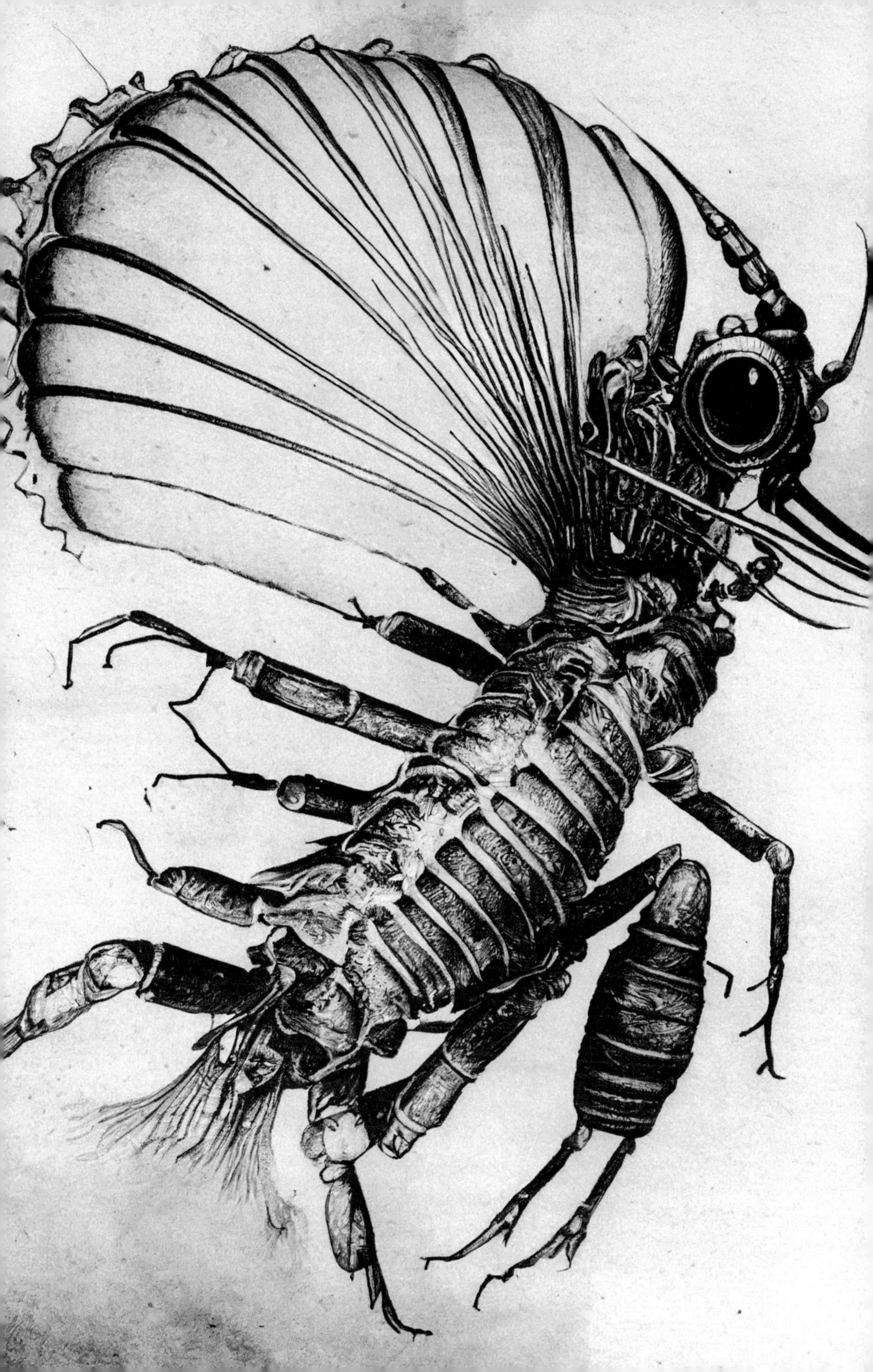

Observations: Egads! I believe I have encountered my first apex predator, and not only was it large—five meters—and fearsome, but it was so reminiscent of a shark, or something that had once been a shark, that I am considering a preposterous hypothesis for which there is little evidence. For the first time since arriving, I am happy to be alone. If I shared my thoughts with anyone, I believe they would laugh me right out of the hab and not let me return. Should I see more evidence of this hypothesis, I will return to it. Until then, I will put it far from my thoughts. While I did not see this beast consume another living being, it is clearly built for the hunt, and its gnarled teeth are designed for shredding flesh. The PSI of Earth's mightiest sharks is a whopping 4,000, just behind that of the mighty Nile Crocodile. I imagine this beast to be quite the same. Despite its size, the creature moved with surprising speed. Its unique triple tail kept it plodding along, but when it wanted to jolt forward, the shark would suck water through the forward orifices on its side and propel the fluid out the rear. A staggering evolution, also reminiscent of cephalopods. On a happy note, the creature paid no interest to the ROV, I assume because its natural prey is not a boxy, yellow-and-black robot with an array of propellers, lights, sensors, and cameras.

Personal Notes: Despite sleeping quite well now, I find myself exhausted this evening. I was so startled by the behemoth's appearance, that I found myself quite shaken. It is one thing to discover curious, playful, and benign creatures. However, it is quite another to encounter something that could sink the hab and make a snack of its sole occupant.

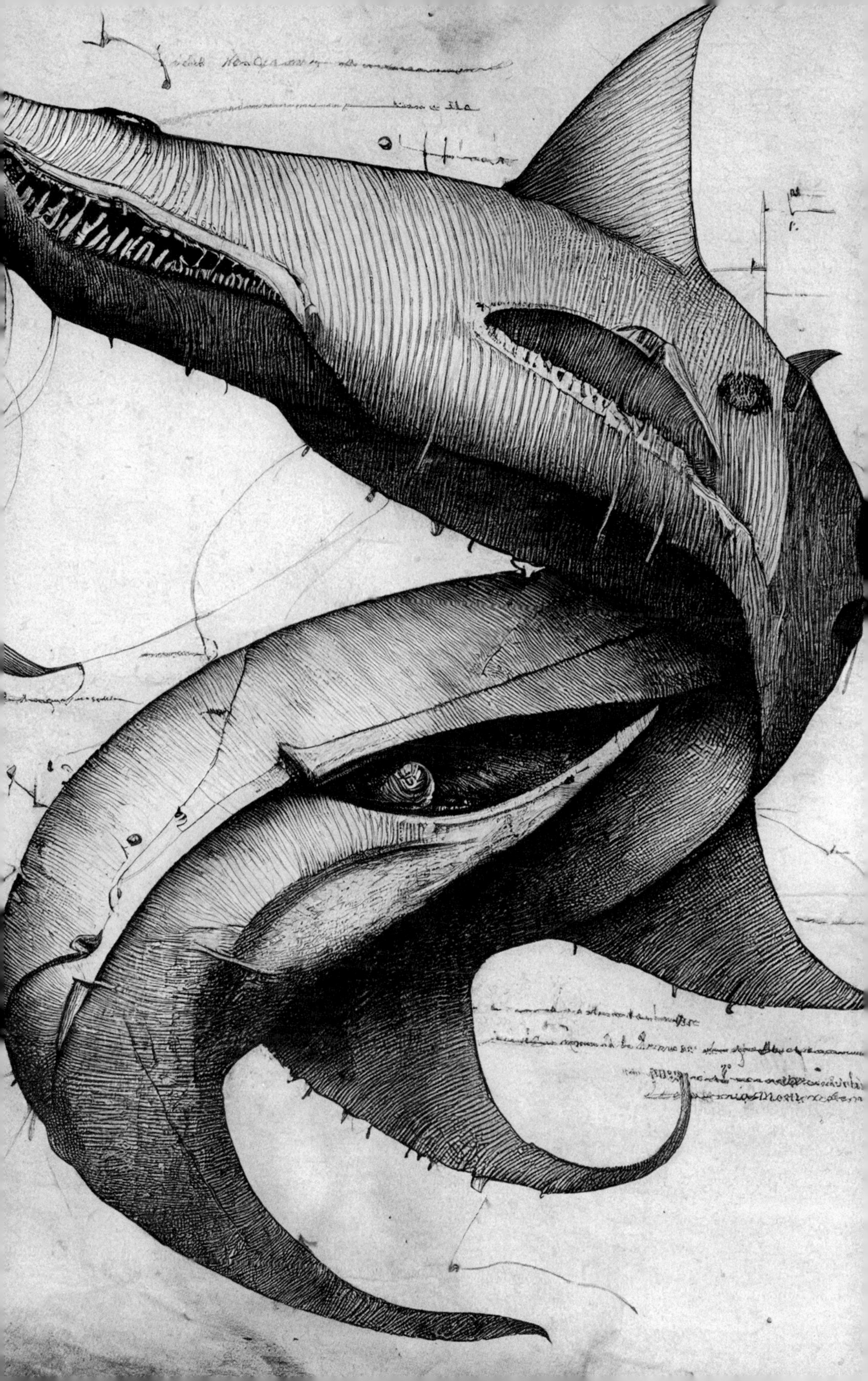

Observations: I can no longer pretend that my thoughts are misguided or the musings of a lonely man with an imagination. This creature...is clearly a biomechanical seahorse. There is no better description. It even tended to its young similarly to its Earth counterpart. Seahorses are an evolutionary oddity. So strangely made and yet perfectly adapted to their habitat. As was this specimen, which clung to swaying vegetation on the sea floor, lazily enjoying the day and its solitary offspring.

Personal Notes: My dear, if it turns out that the sleep aids, or perhaps something in the air, is causing me to hallucinate these things, I hope you will forgive me for becoming a madman. Either way, I wish you could see all this abundant life. Perhaps in the future. Existence on this world is both familiar and strange, but I am encouraged by displays of affection between the shelled lovers, and this parent and child.

Observations: This world is playing games with me. Both jelly fish and cephalopod, this pair of creatures floated past the external cameras during the night. Their passing was brief, but the way the two beings wriggled their tentacles against each other, gave the impression of two old friends, out for a night-time stroll, carrying on about nothing in particular, but enjoying each other's presence. Stunning.

Personal Notes: I have determined to make more of an effort to make friends upon my return. Perhaps I am impressionable at the moment, but I have not felt the kind of kinship these creatures displayed, since I was a boy.

Observations: Upon finishing this drawing, it occurs to me that, despite occupying the majority of a page, the same dimensions as that of my illustration for the five-meter-long...shark, this critter might appear to be similar in size to an insect. Nothing could be closer to the truth. This two-meter-long tank lumbered across the sea floor, vacuuming up everything that it came across. I can only imagine that its mechanical insides are full of dicing blades, grinders, and efficient stomach acid. This arthropod seemed to defecate as quickly as it consumed, which was quite the humorous sight. Unlike other creatures, which fled from the ROV or ignored it, this tank turned and raised its arms in a threat display. I do not think the similarly sized ROV was in any real danger, but I respected this invertebrate's territory and backed away.

Personal Notes: It has become hard to fulfill my promise to you, that we would name anything I found, together, at home. But aside from the few pet names given to my brief friends, I have resisted. Honestly, when I made the promise, I believed it would likely be a suboceanic mound or some such thing. Never did I imagine it would be dozens of creatures in a complicated, robust, and very Earth-like food web.

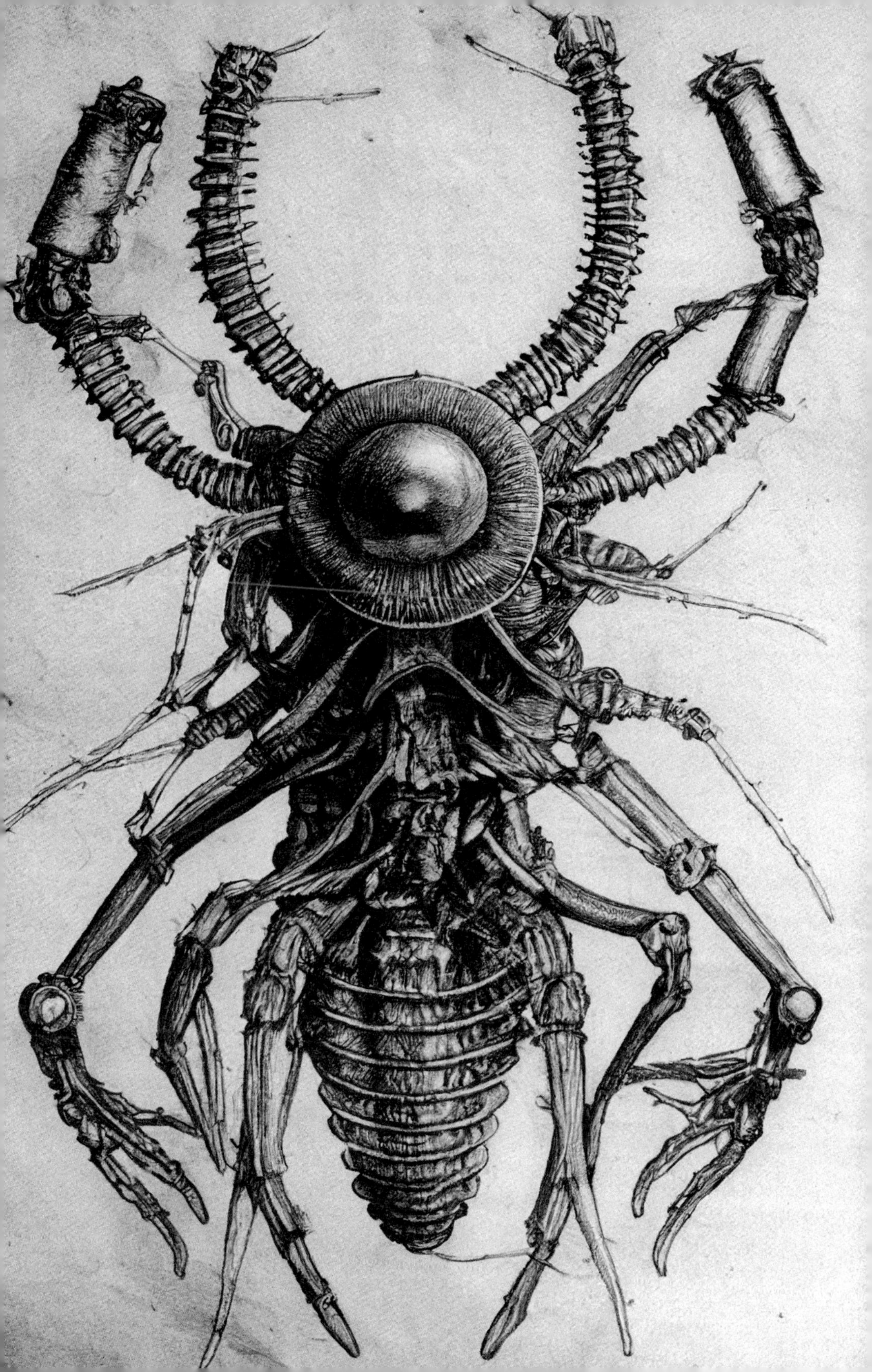

Observations: This item...is a fossil collected from the seabed. I cannot venture how old it is, but given it has fossilized, I imagine it to be ten thousand to many millions of years old. A simple organism.

Personal Notes: I took a break from exploring with the ROV today. I find myself quite overwhelmed by the continuous discovery and the mysterious nature of this planet's very Earth-like denizens. I am going to regroup and approach this problem fresh tomorrow, hopefully with some perspective that allows me to conceive of a more plausible explanation to life evolving on this planet as it did on Earth. Either life's advances are predetermined, which is almost certainly nonsense...or there is my hypothesis, which is at once more ridiculous, and yet more...real.

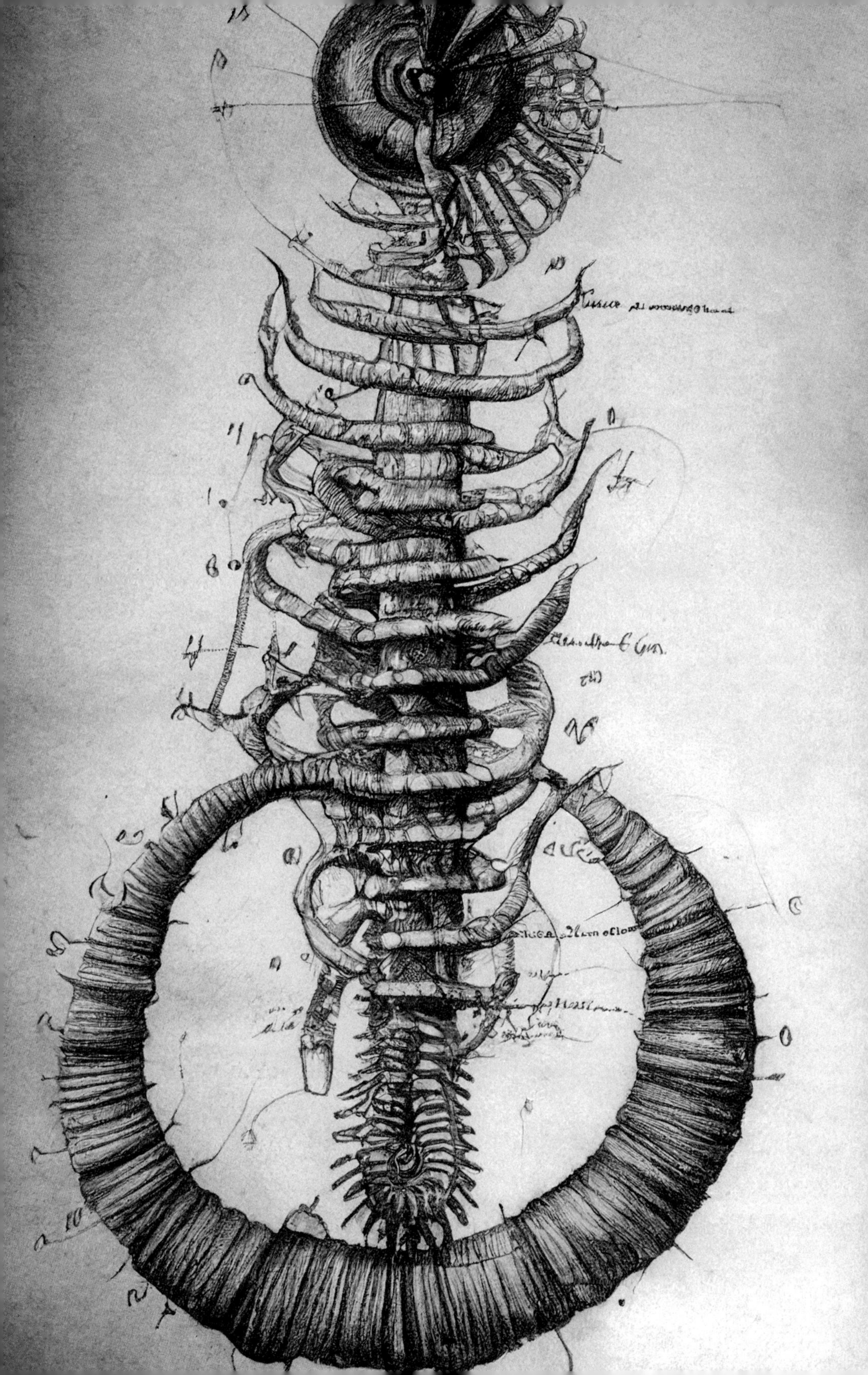

Observations: I must confess that I resorted to vulgarities several times upon discovering this creature with the ROV early this morning. Not only is it very shark-like, but there were also very clear gills just behind the ominous jaw. This world will not let me forget the hypothesis conjured by my mind's eye. Speaking of eyes... The creature's, like that of the great white, are also jet black, and are covered by a white nictitating lens when striking prey, as I learned when not just one, but both sets of jaws attacked the ROV in unison. I do not know if this specimen is an aberration, some kind of mutation, or conjoined twins, but the ease with which it moved through the water and hunted in tandem suggests that the two halves share one mind, which is a rather uncommon adaptation. The ROV survived—with scratches. Thankfully, this species of...shark...was much smaller than the first I came upon.

Personal Notes: Despite my day off and my attempt to approach my observations from an unbiased perspective, I find myself becoming rooted in my hypothesis, which I shall present when no doubt remains.

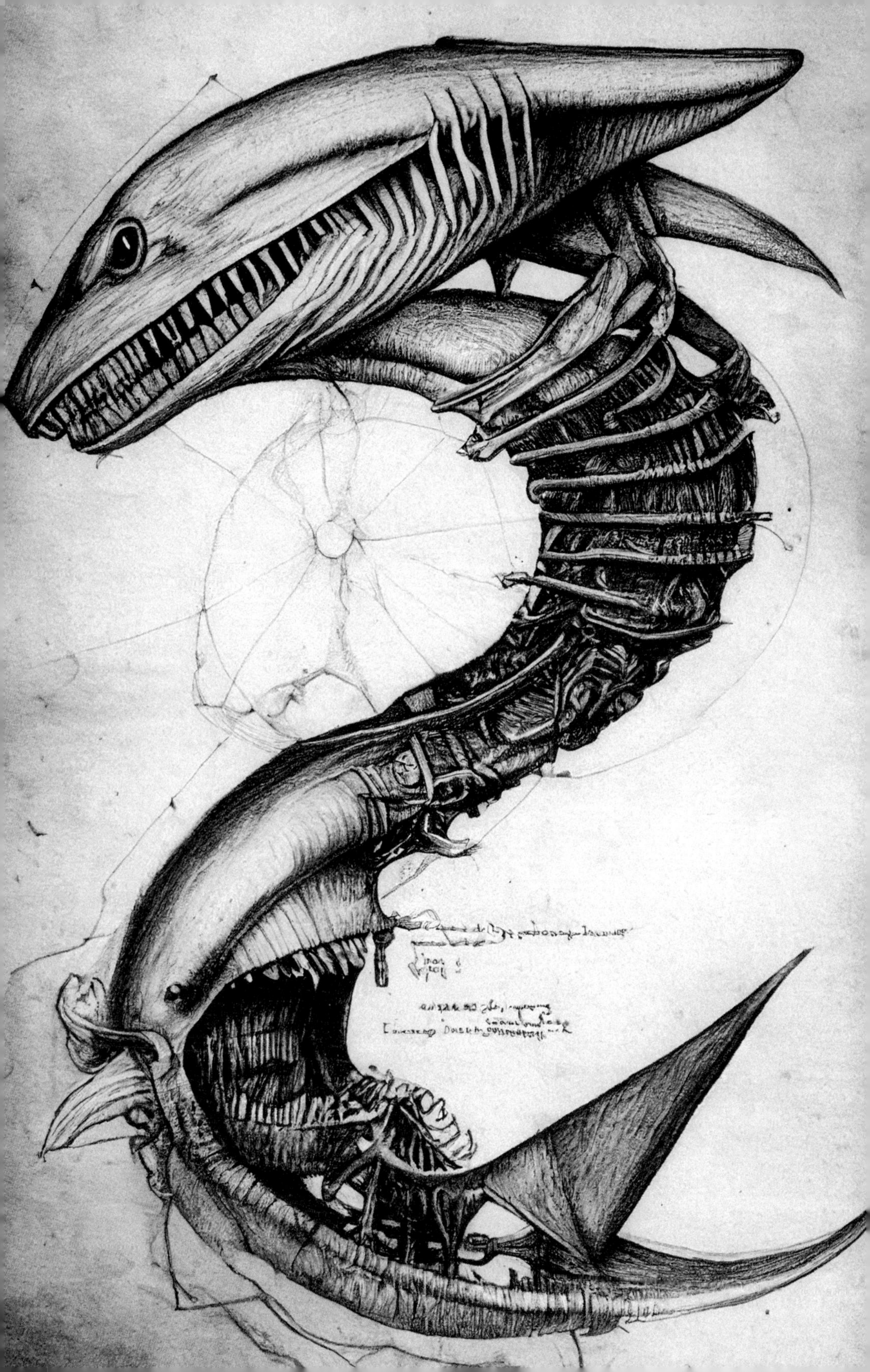

Observations: Another shark? Or a fish? It is hard to say, but it is not even a question I should be mulling over on an alien world. Despite this specimen's blade-like teeth, he was quite mellow. He did not grow wary or aggressive at the ROV's approach. He just continued his slow journey through the sea, happily plodding along. Perhaps it was because of his calm nature, or his canine face, but I felt quite fond of this old gent. That did not stop me from imagining a cross section of his body (the second image). The time for dissection is approaching, though I will not be attempting to capture one of the sharks. They are all too large for me to handle alone, and they are capable of making my study more perilous than academic.

Personal Notes: I have nothing to say. Keeping my cards close to the vest, as they say. I will be wagering a lot when I finally show my hand.

Personal Notes: As I come ever closer to what I think might be groundbreaking discovery or abject insanity, I find myself longing for your company more than ever. While I observed some new species today, they pale in comparison to those recent impossibilities. So, tonight I focus on the subject most pressing on my heart, rather than my mind. My dearest Delilu, by the time you reach this portion of my journal, I hope that I have worked up the courage to ask for your hand in marriage. If I have not, please consider this my asking. While I am confident of your answer, I must confess that, when I think about it, I am brought to a state of intoxicating anxiety, which to a bystander would appear as though I were suffering from the vapors. In case it needs explanation, the drawing of you on the opposite page is both from memory and a projection of the future, when you are reading this journal, hopefully on a page previous to this one, as your demeanor is quite serious. Apologies for the state of your hand. You know how I struggle with them.

Observations: Speechless. Though I am in the habit of talking to myself while making observations, I simply stared at today's visitor. And he stared right back at me with those two hollow, unblinking eyes. Despite obvious differences, this fellow is, without a doubt, the descendant of a cephalopod.

Personal Notes: There. You see? Insanity. How could such a thing be possible? Life on one planet does not evolve from life on another planet...unless, like me, that life ventured to the stars long before humanity stepped out of the jungles.

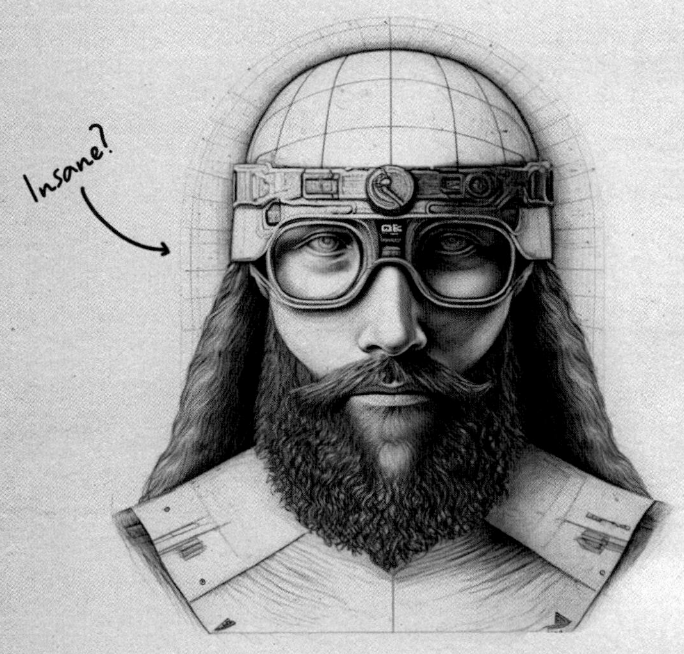

Observations: On any other day, this oddity would have thrilled me. After yesterday's visitor, and the written expression of my hypothesis, I found this specimen to be quite dull. At first. Then I noticed its two cycloptic heads, which I think function together as one. Two sides of the same whole. Its limbs are intriguing as well. This organism is the first I have seen with something resembling hands and fingers. Perhaps once a seahorse. If there were solid earth on this world, I believe this creature might one day drag itself onto dry land.

Personal Notes: Overwhelming exhaustion returns. Sleep is difficult now, even with the pills. I need...a hug. Future missions should probably be made with a dog in tow. Company of any kind would be a blessing. For now, it is just myself and the constant rocking of the waves beneath the hab.

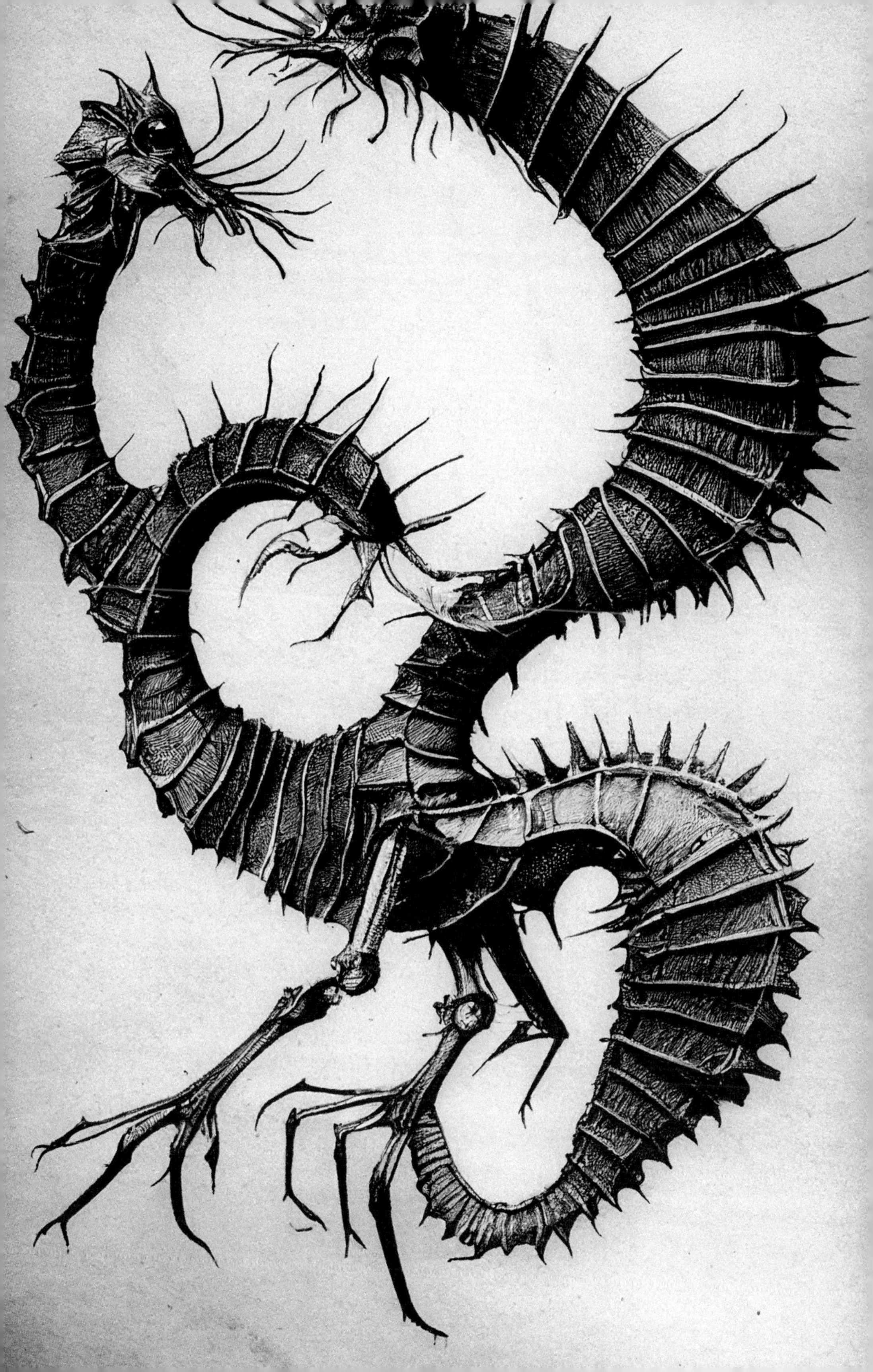

Observations: I am unnerved. It appears word has spread. A second cephalopod came to visit. It seemed to be observing me as much I it. Visually, it is quite horrific, with two independently moving eyes, and an orifice that looks like that of a skull's nose...or lack thereof. After my heart slowed its pace, I came to the conclusion that the creature was actually quite benign, and I set forth a plan to capture this specimen and perform a dissection.

Personal Notes: Nothing today. Focused on work.

Observations: I have done the deed, and despite performing many dissections in the past, this time felt different. I was offended by my actions, as though I had crossed a boundary I did not know existed. That said, there is no longer any doubt that the species on this planet evolved from familiar species that existed on Earth long before humanity. Cellular analysis and genetic testing have confirmed it. I am not insane. I am of sound mind and will likely be remembered by history for millennia to come, second to Darwin. I like to think I will surpass him. What is most shocking about this specimen is that, while it had few biomechanical elements, those that I found appeared to be...implanted, rather than natural growths. Are they foraging trinkets from some ancient civilization? Are they being altered by an existing civilization or...here I go, back to the threshold of madness...are they the existing civilization? If so...God help me.

Personal Notes: None.

Observations: It seems word of my presence continues to spread amidst the cephalopod community. While I have seen plenty of lifeforms lately, these creatures are the only ones that appear to be actively seeking out the ROV. This one looked directly into the lens and cocked its bulbous hood to the side, much like a canine. The limbs on this specimen were all but untouched by machinery, but I believe its true head was hidden beneath a helmet of sorts. Perhaps I am reading more into their visits than I should. For all I know, it is mating season and I am conveniently located in their breeding grounds.

Personal Notes: Nightmares last night. Woke up in a cold sweat. For a moment, I believed myself to be home, and an intruder afoot. But I was alone. Completely alone.

Observations: The devious looking cephalopod followed the ROV today. It kept itself at a distance, but I had no trouble zooming in to record video, take still images, and etch its horrible visage into my memory. Mostly organic this time, I suspect, though it never did turn its back to the ROV. It just...glared. While the corpse of the dissected cephalopod is sealed inside the hab, and frozen, I am beginning to suspect that these other creatures might be looking for it, and their prime suspect at the moment is the ROV. This specimen was quite larger than the others, at three meters. At that size, it would prove a threat to the sharks I have seen and to any human being that decided to take a dip, which I most assuredly will not.

Personal Notes: I find myself confused and a little lost. Stress and anxiety are taking a toll. Sleep comes with drugs, but then fades as I am now stimulated by scientific discovery, curiosity, and a growing fear.

Observations: The ROV was hounded by no less than three cephalopods during its solitary outing today, including the first squid I have seen. It was highly mechanized in a way that suggests my hypothesis might be correct. These creatures are not born this way. They did not evolve to incorporate non-organic elements. They are modifying themselves...and the species around them. The process feels...maniacal, similar to the machinations of the Nazis and Unit 731 during that now ancient war. But it also lends credence to my growing belief that it was cephalopods who once, long ago, evolved to the point where sufficient knowledge was gained and technology developed for their kind to reach for the stars. While their brethren on Earth eventually devolved into the cephalopods we know today, the creatures here—free of competition, thrived along with the many species they took on their voyage. But in all that time, a kind of darkness has overtaken them, and I fear I might have provoked their wrath. These three biomechanical nightmares pursued the ROV with dogged persistence until I had to bring it back, for fear the battery would run out. In doing so, I may have revealed my location.

Personal Notes: The magic of this world has dulled, and I long to leave it more than ever. But I must see this research through. I must... Doubt plagues me, fueled by dread creeping up on me in the night. I hear sounds. Imagine creatures. I am still alone...but also not alone at all.

Observations: Three more. But no longer pursuing the ROV. As I feared, the hab has been discovered. Though too small to pose any real threat—the smallest is no bigger than my forearm, the largest the size of my leg—they swam circles around the hab. On patrol, perhaps. Guards. But I do not think they are trying to keep me inside my prison. I think they are trying to figure out how to get me out...or how to get inside. Cephalopods are quite intelligent on Earth, capable of figuring out complex problems and showing a wide variety of emotions. These creatures have evolved far beyond, and I truly have no idea of what they might be capable. Toward the end of the day, the trio set upon the hab, not so much attacking it as testing it. Their appendages are sharp and rigid. The scraping persisted for an hour, until their curiosity was satisfied. The observer has become the observed. When I think back to what I did to one of theirs, I shiver for fear that they might do the same to me.

Personal Notes: My dear. I cannot shake this terror. It haunts me at night. They are out there. I am sure of it. Bumping and scratching. Watching me sleep through the portal on the floor, waiting for me to blunder before they pounce. My unease has reached a new high, and sleep escapes me once more. Will I see you again? If I am with you when you read this, please take my hand, and do not let go. I will imagine you are doing so now.

Observations: From star up until star down on this fateful day, I was visited by a calm giant. It was fifty meters away and just as long from top to bottom. A behemoth without comparison. Its solitary black eyes faced the hab, unwavering. The creature's tendrils flowed with the water. The gears on its body churned around and around. And the water around...what appear to be transistors...wavers as though heated. I believe this creature to be more machine than living thing. More robot. A cyborg cephalopod, I suppose. But more than that, I cannot shake the feeling that it is here on an official capacity. I am no longer being guarded. I am being judged, my fate decided by a monster that would have no difficulty in crushing the hab and dragging it to the sea floor.

Personal Notes: I cannot sleep. I never did see the goliath squid leave. My view of him simply faded with the star's fall beyond the horizon. I feel...a presence. It is all around, but also moving. Scratches, like nails on a chalkboard, squeal against the hull. They are out there. I know it. All of them, come to get me. I must turn on the lights. I must see for myself. I have determined to do this at once.

Observations: I should not have turned on the lights, for what I saw was far worse than what I had imagined. Looking down through the floor's portal, I turned on the external flood lights and found myself face-to-face with this abomination. Its whole body writhed in an explosion of limbs—and then it was gone, burst out into the depths beyond the reach of my lights. Over the next few hours, I drew what I saw, my nightmare made real, the dread I have been sensing just outside the hull at night. Ten minutes ago, the external lights went out, I know not how. But the scratching and the thumping has returned.

I believe it has come for me.

Personal Notes: My love. My darling. I am sorry. For going on this foolish quest. For not asking for your hand earlier. For...whatever fate befalls me. I hope you can forgive me, and please know that I love you. Know that...

I hear something. Atop the hab. I must go. I love you more than all the life in this universe, and I hope to tell you that in person soon.

Writing in the dark. Hear noises.
Something inside.

My dear,

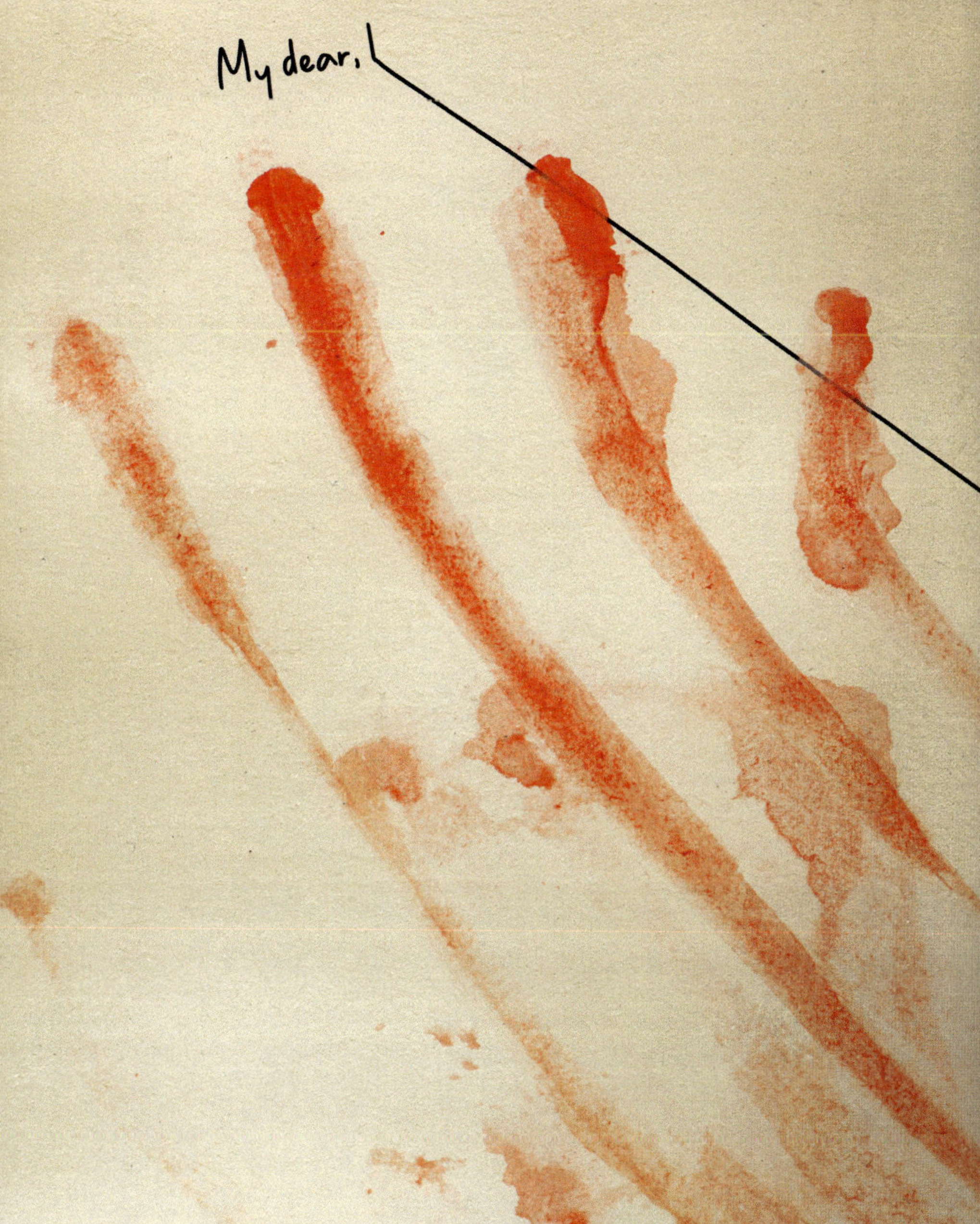

Afterword

This is where the journal concludes. Any reasonable person would assume that the poor doctor met his end at the hands of the creatures he was studying. But I am not a reasonable person. I choose to believe...as can be seen in my fiction...that insurmountable odds can be overcome. Was he killed? Perhaps. Was he taken? There is no way to know.

Not really.

All we can really do is hope that Milos, in all his cosmic wanderings, comes across some other evidence of Dr. Gray's extraordinary life...and that he will bring it to me, to share with you.

Until next time,
Jeremy Robinson

How Was This Book Made
The Author Explains

A few months ago I discovered an A.I. art generator called MidJourney, and I started experimenting with the kinds of images I could create. I quickly became inspired by these crazy drawings of creatures that it was generating from a combination of keywords including: biomechanical, steampunk, and Leonardo Da Vinci. As the images flowed, my imagination went wild and a story came to mind.

I love to experiment with art, writing, and technology so I kind of went nuts, making forty images, arranging them in an order that I felt made sense. Then wrote a story based on that sequence of images. This isn't really a book made with A.I. It's more of a *collaboration* with A.I. My words inspired the images, which in turn inspired the story and the creation of an endearing character. Nearly every part of this book, aside from the font, my words, and the hand at the end was created in MidJourney. That includes the cover, the drawings, the doodles, and even the paper texture behind the text.

After the writing and art were complete, and test readers confirmed Gray's journey was enjoyable, I decided to publish the book and see how the masses responded to it. So here we are with the very first published illustrated novelette created by a merger of human and artificial intelligences. I hope you enjoyed it!

A note on A.I. art: I understand the concerns of artists worried about their art being used to teach A.I. how to draw, paint, etc. Trying to be sensitive to this, I did not use the name of a living artist for any of these images, and primarily used Leonardo Da Vince. For example, one of the prompts I used is:

“scientific pencil drawing on old paper, no color, Leonardo da vinci style, biomechanical, steampunk, mechanical octopus, gears, spikes, goggles, notes”

Give it a try for yourself. See what you get!

—Jeremy

About the Author

Jeremy Robinson is the *New York Times* and #1 Audible bestselling author of over seventy novels and novellas, including *Infinite, The Others,* and *The Dark,* as well as the Jack Sigler thriller series, and *Project Nemesis,* the highest selling, original kaiju novel of all time (which is in development for TV with Chad Stahelski, director of John Wick). Robinson is known for mixing elements of science, history, and mythology, which has earned him the #1 spot in Science Fiction and Action-Adventure, and secured him as the top creature feature author. Many of his novels have been adapted into comic books, optioned for film and TV, and translated into fourteen languages. He lives in New Hampshire with his wife and three children.

Visit him at www.bewareofmonsters.com.

Case Cover design by Jeremy Robinson and Midjourney A.I.
Interior art by Jeremy Robinson and Midjourney A.I.

Visit Jeremy Robinson on the World Wide Web at: www.bewareofmonsters.com.

Made in the USA
Monee, IL
04 March 2023

60c49143-4577-488c-a78f-f172109d83edR01